A LITTLE SPOT LEARNS ONLINE

A STORY ABOUT VIRTUAL CLASSROOM EXPECTATIONS

To my children, Ryan and Anna

This book belongs to:

_____

_____

_____

Hi! My name is SPOT.
I hear you are going to start
learning online, and I'm
here to help!

Absolutely!
Learning virtually or online, is like learning at school, but it just feels a little different.

Instead of LEARNING in a physical classroom at school...

You will be LEARNING on a computer in a
virtual classroom at home! You will still see your teacher
and all the kids in your class!

And they will be able to see you, too!

So you definitely don't want to be in your pajamas!

Joining a virtual class is like going to school, so you should wear something comfortable and appropriate.

This will help you get your mind ready to learn and help you stay on schedule, too!

EAT BEFORE

you join your class online!

You don't want a grumbling stomach when you are trying to learn.

Eating while you're in a virtual classroom can be a distraction, not only to you, but to your teacher and classmates too! Don't worry. Your teacher will have scheduled snack breaks.

Be ORGANIZED and PREPARED.

You should avoid getting up and leaving your classroom session. Having a water bottle nearby is a great idea, in case you get thirsty.

Make sure you have the school supplies that your teacher recommends in close reach as well.

And the biggest thing of all...

...before you join your virtual class!

Find a GOOD PLACE TO SIT.

You might want to sit on the floor or
the couch, but this can get uncomfortable.

When you are uncomfortable, you move around A LOT! Try
sitting on a chair, this will help you stay upright
and focused.

If you don't have a desk chair, a dining room chair works, too!

Create a **QUIET SPACE.**
A place with few distractions can make learning easier.

And...

LOOK BEHIND YOU!

Teachers and students can see what is in the background
of your computer camera, so make sure that is appropriate, too!

Now...

LOOK AROUND YOU!

Make sure all
your toys are
put away...

all the food is
out of reach...

and any pets are in another room.

Always try to be
ON TIME.

When you are ON TIME,
it shows RESPECT for
your teacher and that you
are RESPONSIBLE.

Sometimes there can be technical problems, so always try to join a virtual class 5 MINUTES early. This way an adult can make sure your computer is fully charged, your camera works, and your microphone is muted.

Now you are....

READY TO LEARN!

You will be able to LEARN the best when your:

When you have something to say, make sure you:

Raise your hand and wait your turn.

Wow! You both are working so hard!

I hope I've helped make this experience a little easier.
I can't wait to see how much you LEARN and how much FUN
you have with ONLINE LEARNING!

Also available:

A Little SPOT Stays HOME is a companion to A Little SPOT Learns Online. This story helps children understand viruses and why it is important to stay home when you are sick.

For free printables and worksheets that go along with these books, visit www.dianealber.com

Made in the USA
Columbia, SC
25 September 2020

21570452R00020